Cinderella

Retold and illustrated by
Ruth Sanderson

LB
1837

Little, Brown and Company
Boston New York London

For Rebecca and Matt
and Vivian Ruth

First Edition

This retelling is based on the classic French version by Charles Perrault and includes
elements such as the white bird from the Brothers Grimm.

Library of Congress Cataloging-in-Publication Data
Sanderson, Ruth.
    Cinderella / retold and illustrated by Ruth Sanderson. — 1st ed.
        p. cm.
    Summary: Although she is mistreated by her stepmother and stepsisters, a kindhearted young woman
manages to attend the palace ball with the help of her fairy godmother.
    ISBN 0-316-77965-2
    [1. Fairy tales. 2. Folklore.] I. Cinderella. English. II. Title.

PZ8.S253 Ci 2002
398.2'0944'02—dc21   00-066419

10 9 8 7 6 5 4 3 2 1

TWP

Printed in Singapore

The illustrations for this book were done in oils on primed watercolor paper.
The text was set in Truesdell, and the display type is Poppl-Exquisit.

Once upon a time there was a gentleman who, after his beloved first wife died, married a widow with two daughters. When his new wife and stepdaughters arrived at his home and met his only daughter, they hated her at once, for they were vain and jealous creatures.

The new stepmother sent the poor girl to live in the kitchen and thrust upon her all the lowly tasks in the house — cleaning, doing laundry, weeding the gardens, cooking, and sewing. Indeed, the young girl became a servant, running from morning till night, from one task to the next, until she fell into an exhausted heap upon the kitchen hearth at the end of the day.

"Look," said one stepsister, peering into the kitchen one morning and finding the girl still asleep in the ashes. "What a smutty, cinder-covered mess!"

"Let's call her Cinderella," suggested the other.

"Cinderella! Cinderella!" they chanted together, laughing at the joke they had made at her expense.

Cinderella's father said nothing of his daughter's new circumstances, for he was totally ruled by his new wife. One day, as he was leaving to go to town, he asked his stepdaughters if they would like a trinket from the town fair.

"I want a pearl necklace," said the elder.

"I want a pink satin gown," demanded the other.

"And you, my daughter?" the father asked Cinderella sheepishly, for he was ashamed of how she was treated and wished to make amends in some way.

"The first twig, Father, that brushes against your hat on the way home," Cinderella said.

And so he brought his stepdaughters expensive pearls and a fancy new gown. To Cinderella he gave what she had requested, a little hazel twig. As her stepsisters were admiring their fine gifts, Cinderella took the hazel twig out to the garden and planted it next to a beautiful white rosebush. Her mother had especially loved roses.

Cinderella wept as she thought of her mother, and as she cried her tears watered the hazel twig. At once the little branch began to grow and grow, and in no time a beautiful hazel tree stood in its place. A white bird flew onto one branch and sang a tune so lovely and sweet that it eased the sadness in Cinderella's heart. From that day on, Cinderella brought the bird bits of stale bread, and every day it sang for her and ate the bread out of her hand.

Time passed and Cinderella became accustomed to her hard labor, almost forgetting that she, too, had once been a fine young lady with handsome clothes and a soft bed to sleep in.

Now, it happened that the king's son was giving a grand ball soon, and all the eligible young ladies of the kingdom were invited.

"Cinderella, where is my fan?" "Where are my blue shoes?" "Are my best petticoats clean?" "Fix my hair! Fetch my fan! Hurry! Run! You are too lazy for words!" Cinderella's stepsisters kept up in this manner for hours, trying to prepare themselves for the ball. Cinderella patiently did everything they asked. Then she ran downstairs and begged her stepmother to allow her to attend the ball as well.

"What?! You, a dirty kitchen wench, would be laughed out of the ball!"

But Cinderella persisted until finally her stepmother grabbed a bowl of lentils from the table and angrily tossed them into the fireplace ashes.

"If you can put all those lentils back into the bowl in two hours, you may go to the ball," she said cruelly. Then she stalked out of the room.

Knowing the task was hopeless, Cinderella despaired. But then the white bird from the hazel tree appeared at the open window.

"Oh, sweet bird," said Cinderella, "if only you could help me. There are so many lentils in the ashes, and I need to pick them all out in two hours' time so I can go to the ball!"

At once, the bird began to sing and was soon joined by other birds from the garden. Starlings, doves, and finches flew in the window and alighted among the ashes, picking out the lentils and returning them to the dish that Cinderella held.

When all the lentils were back in the bowl, Cinderella ran to show her stepmother, who was preparing to leave for the ball with her daughters.

"Foolish girl," said the stepmother. "Did you think I was serious? How could you go to the ball with no proper clothes?" And Cinderella was left on the doorstep as her stepmother and stepsisters brushed past her to the coach waiting outside.

As Cinderella watched with longing, their coach disappeared out the gate. She went to the garden and sank onto the stone bench under the hazel tree. The white bird was nowhere in sight. Her unhappiness deepened. Had she no friend in the world?

11

"So, you want to go to the ball?" said a voice behind her. Cinderella looked around and was astonished to see a beautiful fairy standing by the hazel tree. She had seen all that had happened.

"What are you waiting for, Cinderella? Fetch me the largest pumpkin from your garden."

Cinderella found a huge pumpkin and rolled it out of the garden and onto the driveway. With a touch of her magic wand, the fairy transformed the pumpkin into a golden coach.

"Now fetch me the mousetrap and we'll see about some horses," she said.

There were six gray mice in the trap, and as Cinderella let them out, her
fairy godmother changed them one by one into beautiful dapple-gray carriage
horses.

"What about a coachman?" asked Cinderella. "I think I saw a big, plump rat
in the rat trap."

"A good idea," said her fairy godmother. "Go and fetch it."

The rat made a fine coachman, with a long mustache, and he immediately began to harness the horses to the coach as though he had been doing it for years.

Then Cinderella's fairy godmother said, "Look in the garden behind the watering pot. I imagine there might be a few lizards there that would make excellent footmen." And so, with a touch of the magic wand, the lizards became footmen and took their place on the back of the carriage.

Cinderella was thrilled. Then she looked down at her own ragged appearance.

"Ah, not to worry, my dear," said her fairy godmother kindly. And with a wave of her wand, she transformed Cinderella's rags into a gown of golden silk, embroidered with pearls. As Cinderella looked down to admire the beautiful gown, she noticed that upon her feet were dainty slippers made entirely of glass.

"Now you are ready to go to the ball," said the fairy. "But mind you, this enchantment lasts only till midnight. Then coach turns to pumpkin, horses back to mice, coachman to rat, footmen to lizards, and your finery back to rags. You must leave the ball before midnight! Do not forget."

Cinderella promised, and thanked her fairy godmother. The golden coach carried her swiftly to the king's palace.

When Cinderella entered the grand hall, everyone stopped dancing, stopped talking, and stared, for she was dazzling in her splendid gown. Word spread quickly that a beautiful, unknown princess had arrived. But it was Cinderella's

sweet face that engaged the prince. He immediately asked her to dance, and would have no other partner the whole evening long. As they talked and laughed, Cinderella felt happy for the first time in years.

The evening passed so quickly that Cinderella forgot her promise until
the clock began to strike midnight. *Bong . . . Bong . . . Bong . . . Bong . . .*

Cinderella ran from the room and dashed down the palace stairs so quickly that she stumbled and lost one of her slippers.

The shadow of the palace wall hid her as the last stroke of midnight rang out, and then Cinderella slipped out the gate, dressed once again in her rags. Six mice scurried past her, followed by the rat and the lizards. The pumpkin rolled to the edge of the road and then into a ditch, where it shattered.

Cinderella walked slowly home, as if in a dream.

The next day, the prince found the glass slipper on the stairs and declared he would have no bride other than the one whose foot fit that shoe. And so began a search of the entire kingdom. Days passed, but the prince and his servant could not find the lady whose foot fit the glass slipper. The last house they stopped at was Cinderella's.

The prince and his servant were shown into the drawing room, where Cinderella's stepsisters awaited. First the elder tried to get her huge toes into the slipper, without success. Then the younger sister tried. She managed to get her toes in, but however much she pushed, she could not force her heel into the shoe.

"Are there no other young ladies in this house?" asked the prince.

"There are none," said Cinderella's stepmother. "Just a dirty cinder-wench who works in the kitchen." Cinderella's father frowned but said nothing.

"Who is that in the garden, then?" asked the prince, staring out the window.

Cinderella's father had kept silent for fear of angering his wife, but the sight of his daughter in the sunlit rose garden reminded him so much of his first wife that he took courage and spoke.

"That is my daughter," he said. "She is beautiful, isn't she?" Then he led the prince outside, leaving his wife and stepdaughters spluttering and, for once, speechless.

In spite of her ragged dress, the prince recognized Cinderella immediately. She sat on the garden bench, and the prince himself knelt to try the glass slipper on her foot. It fit perfectly.

Then Cinderella reached into her pocket, took out a matching slipper, and put it on as well.

As Cinderella stood up, the sound of birdsong suddenly
filled the air. Soon she was surrounded by fluttering wings and
joyful chirping as all the birds in the garden flocked around her.
The white bird settled on her outstretched hand. Instantly
Cinderella's dress became a gown of shimmering silk. It was a final gift
from her fairy godmother.

Cinderella's stepsisters ran into the garden, for they now recognized her as
the beautiful young lady they had seen at the ball. They fell down at her feet and
begged her pardon for their poor treatment of her, and being a kindhearted soul,
Cinderella forgave them at once.

The prince and Cinderella departed in a splendid coach to return to the
palace to make their wedding plans. It soon became apparent that Cinderella's
stepmother and stepsisters would not be in attendance, however. For as the
coach went out the gate, the birds in the garden flew at the women with fury,

pecking at them until they fled for their lives back into the house. And there
they remained for the rest of their days, for the birds were constantly on guard,
and the women could not set so much as one foot out the door.

As for Cinderella and the prince, they lived happily ever after.